Easy Books

YANKEE STADIUM

W9-AZY-674

BLOOM'S

Beatrice Farms

Mr. Clark Kent
The Daily Planet
Metropolis

TELL ME A TRUDY

TELL ME A TRUDY

LORE SEGAL

PICTURES BY

ROSEMARY WELLS

FARRAR · STRAUS · GIROUX

NEW YORK

For Priscilla and Claire / L.S.

For Sheldon Fogelman / R.W.

CONTENTS

TRUDY AND THE COPYCATS

TRUDY AND THE DUMP TRUCK

TRUDY AND SUPERMAN

TRUDY AND THE COPYCATS

"Now get washed, and hurry up to bed," said Martha's mother.

"May I have a glass of milk?" asked Martha.

"Certainly," her mother said.

"And while I'm drinking it," said Martha, "you tell me a Trudy."

Once upon a time (*said her mother*) there was a girl whose name was Gertrude but they called her Trudy and she had a brother. His name was Jacob. They had a father and a mother, and the mother said, "Hurry up to bed, everybody!" and Trudy said, "Hurry up to bed, everybody!" and Trudy's mother said, "Oh no, not that, I can't bear it!" and Trudy said, "Oh no, not that, I can't bear it!" and Jacob said, "Me too!"

"Not you too, Jacob!" cried his mother.

"Not you too, Jacob!" cried Trudy.

"Harry!" said Trudy's mother. "The children are copycatting me!"

"We'll soon put a stop to that," said Trudy's father. "I'm going to copycat the children."

"We'll soon put a stop to that," said Trudy. "I'm going to copycat the children."

"Me too!" said Jacob.

Trudy's mother sat down. "I think I'm going to cry," she said and started to laugh.

"I think I'm going to cry," said Trudy.

"I'm going to cry," said Trudy's father.

"Me too," said Jacob, and they laughed and they laughed and they laughed.

"There's the doorbell," said Trudy's mother.

"There's the doorbell," said Trudy and her father, and you know what Jacob said.

It was Grandma.

"Mother!" cried Trudy's mother. "Harry and the children are copycatting me and they won't go to bed when I tell them." She kissed Grandma and so did Trudy and so did her father.

"Hey, me too!" cried Jacob.

"You know what I'm going to do?" said Grandma. "I'm going into the bedroom."

"You know what I'm going to do?" said Trudy. "I'm going into the bedroom."

"And me too," said Jacob.

"Me too," said Trudy's mother. "I'm tired!"

"Me too!" said Trudy's father.

"I think I'll just take off my shoes," said Grandma.

"And I'm just going to take *my* shoes off," said Trudy.

"And me too!" said Jacob.

"I think I'll just take my shoes off and stretch out on the bed awhile," Trudy's mother said.

"Oh, me *too*," said Trudy's father.

"I'm tired," said Grandma. "Maybe I'll just stretch out on this bed here."

"And I'll stretch out beside you," said Trudy.

"And you stretch out too, Jacob," said Grandma. "Who's going to turn out the light?"

"Me, I will," said Jacob.

"Let's turn the light out," said Trudy's father.
"I will," said Trudy's mother. "Good night, Harry."
"Good night, dear," said Trudy's father.

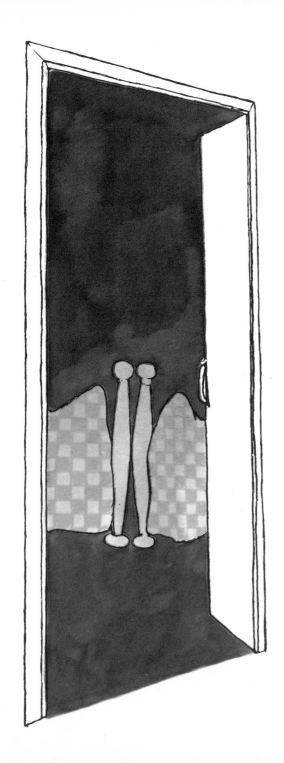

"Have a good night, everybody," said Grandma.
"You too, Grandma," said Trudy.
"And me too," said Jacob.

TRUDY AND THE DUMP TRUCK

"Tell me a Trudy," said Martha.

"I just told you one," said her mother.

"So tell me another," said Martha. "Go on."

Once upon a time (*said her mother*) there was a child whose name was Gertrude but they called her Trudy. She had a little brother called Jacob and they had a father. The father had a sister who had a baby whose name was Leonard who had a brand-new dump truck. It was red.

"I want it," said Jacob.

"Here's a nice bucket for you, Jacob," said Aunt Shirley. "And a quarter for you, Trudy, to buy whatever you want."

"Thank you, Aunt Shirley," said Trudy. "Say 'Thank you for the nice bucket,' Jacob!" But Jacob said, "I already got a bucket," and Jacob's father said, "Shush, Jacob. Why don't we all go for a nice walk in the park?"

So Trudy put her quarter in her pocketbook, and Jacob said, "I'll carry the dump truck." Leonard said, "It's *my* dump truck," and Aunt Shirley said, "Let Jacob play with it, Leonard, you've got to share," and Jacob's father said, "Give it back, Jacob, he's only a baby."

In the park, Trudy sat on the bench and listened to the grownups having a conversation. Jacob took Leonard's dump truck and said, "Here's where you put the dirt in and here's where you dump it out," and Leonard said, "It's mine, and I'm only a baby." Jacob's father said, "Come on, children, no fighting," and Aunt Shirley said, "Share nicely."

Trudy said, "Hey, Jacob, can Leonard put dirt in your bucket?"

"Okay. And you can dump the bucket in the dump truck," Jacob said to Trudy.

"And you can dump it out," Leonard said to Jacob.

"Hey, Daddy," said Trudy. "We're sharing."

"Good for you," said her father.

"And you can keep my bucket, Leonard," said Jacob.

"And you can keep my dump truck," said Leonard.
"Mommy, I'm letting Jacob keep my dump truck."

"He can borrow it," Aunt Shirley said. "And afterwards
you give it back to Leonard, okay, Jacob?"

"No," said Leonard. "He can keep it. It's his dump truck."

"No, dear, it's not," said Aunt Shirley. "It's a brand-new dump truck! I bought it for *you*."

"And I'm giving it to Jacob," said Leonard.

"And I'm giving him my nice new bucket," said Jacob.

"That's right, Shirley. *Their* toys, that they can do with whatever they like!"

"You know what that dump truck cost me?" cried Aunt Shirley.

"You wanted them to share, Shirley!" said Trudy's father.

"Come on, Daddy," said Trudy, "no fighting. You give Aunt Shirley back her dump truck and I'll buy everybody a pretzel."

"Five pretzels, please," Trudy said to the pretzel man. But he said, "Pretzels are three for a quarter, miss," so Aunt Shirley had to share with Trudy's daddy and Jacob shared with Leonard. "And I get a whole one to myself," said Trudy, "because it's my quarter."

TRUDY AND SUPERMAN

"Is Superman real, Daddy?" Martha asked her father.

"I'm watching the news, Martha," her father said.

"Daddy," Martha asked, "are there really bad guys?"

"Are there ever," said her father.

"Is there really a Trudy?" Martha asked.

"I'll tell you a story," her father answered.

Once upon a time (*her father said*) there was a girl called Gertrude but they called her Trudy and she had a brother whose name was Jacob and a mother who was always telling them to get washed and hurry up to bed, but there were robbers behind the bathroom door, or maybe back of the shower curtain or hiding under her father's terry-cloth robe, and Trudy didn't want to go in there.

So she wrote Superman a letter.

Mr. Clark Kent
The Daily Planet
Metropolis

Dear Superman,
How Are you? I AM Fine. PLEAse come And Get Rid of the Robbers in our BATHROOM in the tub or under my Daddy's BAthrobe or Behind the Door. JACOB SAYS MAYBE MARTiANS. Love, TRUDY

Next day the doorbell rang. It was Superman, extremely handsome even with his glasses on. He said, "I got your letter."

"I've seen you lots of times," said Jacob, "in our TV."

"Is there some place I can change?" asked Superman.

"You can use the bathroom," said Trudy, but Superman said he didn't know if he ought to go in there in his regular clothes, and Trudy said, "You'll be all right, Superman. There's nothing wrong with our bathroom till it gets dark."

Jacob said, "I've seen you fly in the TV."

When Superman had changed, Trudy took him in the living room and said, "This is Superman. He's come about the bathroom."

"Won't you have a chair," said Trudy's mother.

"We're watching the news," said Trudy's father. "Terrible, what with one thing after another, and now robbers in our bathroom."

"You always think it only happens to other people," said Trudy's mother.

When it got dark, Superman said, "Okay. Now. I want you all to stand clear, there may be trouble," and he went into the bathroom.

"Nobody behind the door," he called out to them.

"How about the tub?" Trudy called in.

"No," Superman called out. "I'm looking through the shower curtain with my X-ray vision and there's nothing there. Okay. Now I will push my fist of steel through your father's terry-cloth robe."

There was a whoop, a whump, a short, sharp scuffle, and the crash of glass, and Superman opened the door and came out.

"Four of them," he said. "I'm sorry about the window."

"Don't mention it," said Trudy's mother. "We're just so grateful!"

"You were right," said Superman, shaking Jacob's hand. "Martians. They won't bother you any more," he told Trudy.

"Won't you stay and have a little supper, Superman?" Trudy's mother asked, but Superman said thank you very much, he couldn't even take the time to put his street clothes on,

what with all the trouble downtown. He said goodbye and
flew out the window.

"Now get washed, you two, and hurry up to bed, just look at the time," Trudy's mother said.

"Trudy?" said Jacob.

"What?" Trudy said.

"Was that really Superman?"

"Well," Trudy said, "the bad guys in the bathroom are all gone."